Patti

A true story Illustrated and written by
Xiao Ch'iao

Copyright © 2001 Christian Focus Publications, Geanies House, Fearn Tain
Ross-shire, IV20 1TW, Scotland, U.K.,
www.christianfocus.com   ISBN: 1-85792-557-2
Co-published with OMF International, Borough Green,
Sevenoaks, Kent, TN15 8BG, www.omf.org.uk
Printed in Singapore

The phonetic spelling of Weegor is used in this book instead of the actual spelling of Uighur. This is for ease of pronunciation for young readers.

Good Books with the Real Message of Hope

OMF

In Xinjiang, China, where there is plenty of singing and dancing, lives Pattigool. She has lived there all her life. Her parents have lived there all their lives, and her grandparents, great grandparents and even her great, great grandparents. All her relatives live nearby.

Patti, as her friends call her, lives in the countryside with her father and mother, one older sister and one older brother. Their house is a traditional Weegor house. It has three rooms and a courtyard in front.

The left room is the family room, where the family watches television, eats and sleeps. Everyone sleeps in the same room on the *kang* (a raised platform covered with rugs). Each evening, they roll out the *korpa* (mattresses) *yot kan* (blankets) and *yastuk* (pillows). In the daytime, these things are rolled-up and stacked against the wall.

The room on the right is the *meh man hana* (livingroom). When guests come over, they are entertained in this room. They are invited to sit on the platform. A cloth is spread out in front of the guests. Then a tall stack of *nan* (bread) and little dishes of candies and nuts are placed on the cloth. *Chai* (tea) is served in a bowl and the guests are invited to enjoy all that is before them.

The centre room is an all purpose room.
Sometimes it's where people sleep. Sometimes
it's where food is cooked. Sometimes it is a
storage place. When Patti's sister got married,
she sat on a platform in the centre room for six
hours to greet all the neighbourhood women.
During the winter, all the cooking is done over
the coal stove in the centre room.

In Patti's village everyone is *Weegor*. Weegors like eating meat like mutton or lamb with *lah mun* (long noodles). Weegors don't eat pork. They rinse their hands three times before eating. All of the men and boys wear *doppa* (hats) and a *bichak* (knife). Every Friday afternoon, they go to the local mosque to pray.

When they pray, they all face west towards Saudi Arabia. This is because most Weegors are *Muslims*. The women and girls don't go to the mosque because only men and boys are allowed into the mosque. All the women wear *koy nek* (dresses) and *shar pa* (head scarves).

Except for the few carpenters and one bicycle repairman, everyone in Patti's town is a farmer. Patti's father is a wheat farmer. He has no truck, just a long-handled shovel.

Patti loves to dance. Her town is full of musicians, singers and dancers. Patti's feet love to stomp and turn; her hands to sway and flow with music. Patti's mother is a master *dombala* (a Weegor guitar) player. At night after all the work is done she will sing and play Weegor folk songs with Patti dancing along.

One day Patti's beloved father got very, very sick. He lay in bed all day long for a year. He got thinner and thinner. Sometimes Patti would shout at her father for being so sick. She was scared. She was afraid he would die. When he did die, her grandfather also died on the very same day. Patti's mother was so upset that she smashed her dombala to pieces. Patti just felt so bad for screaming at her father.

From that day on, there was no more singing or dancing in their family. Even their relatives and neighbours kept away because they thought Patti's family had bad *jinn* (evil spirits).

When Patti was 18 years old, she left home for college. Unlike her village, this city had many *Han* people. The Han are Chinese people who speak a language called Mandarin and not the Weegor language like Patti. In college all classes are taught in Mandarin which Patti had learnt in primary school.

Patti lived at the college. She shared a small *yatak* (dorm room) with seven other girls. Each girl had a bunk-bed with space at the end for a large suitcase. There was no room for anything else. Washbasins and shoes were kept under the lower bunks. Patti would stay here for the next three years. Living with all these girls was fun.

But at nights Patti would often be haunted by terrible nightmares. In her dreams, she saw her father. He was so thin, sickly and ugly. These nightmares made Patti very upset. She tried putting a knife under her pillow to keep the evil spirits from bringing those frightening dreams to her. But it did not work.

In the holidays Patti went home. She asked her
mother, 'How can I stop the nightmares?' Her
mother went to an Islamic religious teacher for
help. The teacher wrote religious words in Arabic
on a tiny piece of paper, rolled it up and put it in
a tiny tube. He prayed over it and said, 'If your
daughter wears this around her neck, the
nightmares will stop.'

Patti brought the tiny tube back to college.
'Now everything is going to be fine', she thought.
But not only did the nightmares continue, Patti
also became very sick.

She went to the school's hospital. The doctor gave her some medicine, but it did not make her feel any better. She could not sleep at all. After a few sleepless nights, unexpectedly, a fellow student appeared in her dorm.

Patti had met this Han student before, but never talked to her much. The student announced 'I heard you are sick. I have no classes today, so I will stay with you and help you.' While the other dorm mates left for classes, the visiting student pulled up a stool and sat with Patti for the rest of the day.

The student shared some interesting stories to entertain Patti. She told Patti about her family; her mother is a clerk, her dad is a teacher, and her brother is a scientist. She sang some lovely songs about love, faith and hope. Her gentle voice and caring helped Patti to fall asleep.

By evening, her dorm mates returned from classes. So the kind student got up to leave. Patti awoke just in time to say *rah met* (thank you). Before the student left, she asked Patti if she could pray for her.

'Pray?' thought Patti, 'I didn't know Han people prayed.' Patti was puzzled. She let the Han student pray because she had been so kind to her. It was an interesting prayer; not long and recited like the Weegor prayers. It used simple words, asking God to help Patti feel better. That night, Patti slept peacefully; no nightmares and very little pain. Within days, Patti was better.

'Tell me about that Han girl,' Patti asked someone who was a close friend of the Han student. Patti found out that the Han student was a Christian and that Christians believe God loves them and cares for them. That was very different from the Weegors' belief in God. So together with her dorm mate, Patti got to know this Christian student.

Patti asked the Christian student many questions. 'Weegors have the Koran. How is the Koran different from your Christian Bible?' After a while, Patti knew that she wanted a relationship with a loving God. She wanted to follow the teachings of Jesus Christ.

But then she would be a Christian. 'How would my mother react if I told her I had become a Christian?' Patti asked the kind student. 'She may not care,' the kind student replied, 'but she might beat you.'

Some Muslims can get angry if other Muslims change their religion. The kind student encouraged Patti not to fear but to trust in Jesus Christ's ability to protect her and care for her.

Patti did not have the courage to become a
Christian. All her Weegor friends, family and
relatives were Muslims. The school had also
threatened and kicked out students for
practising a different religion. Patti imagined
herself facing all kinds of problems if she followed
Jesus Christ.

But Jesus saw Patti's fears. So He arranged for Patti to bump into two other Weegor Christians. She had never met them before or even heard of them. Nor had they ever heard of Patti. It was so amazing how God arranged all the details so that Patti could gain courage from the testimonies of her new friends. God gave Patti the courage to follow Him.

TWO YEARS LATER

Patti's sister and her sister's husband now believe in Jesus too. Patti has had troubles and threats from teachers and police but God's love makes it worth it.

God is with Patti always. Every day he protects her from evil and gives her his courage. He brings other Christians into her life to help her.

Patti now wants to help others to believe in Jesus and to become strong in their faith. Jesus Christ sees and He cares.

"I will make you fruitful and will increase your numbers. I will make you a community of peoples, and I will give this land as an everlasting possession to your descendants after you." Genesis 48:4

Pray for China

China Ministries International has a Prayer Club that you can join.
Contact them at : CMI, 7 Landsdowne Crescent,
Portrush, Co. Antrim, BT56 8AY

Pray for Xinjiang

New words and foreign language words

Xinjiang: The area of China that Patti comes from
Weegor: The tribe of people that Patti belongs to. The proper spelling of this word is Uighur. It is pronounced Weegor
Han: Another group of Chinese people who speak the Mandarin language
Muslim: Someone who follows the teachings of Islam
Mosque: The place where Muslims go to worship
Koran: A book of Muslim laws and teaching
Christian: Someone who believes and trusts in the Lord Jesus Christ
Bible: God's word. A book where God tells you about himself
Kan: A raised platform covered with rugs
Korpa: Mattresses
Yot kan: Blankets
Yastuk: Pillows
Meh man hana: Living room
Nan: Bread
Chia: Tea
Lah mun: Long noodles
Doppa: Hats
Bichak: Knife
Koy nek: Dresses
Shar pa: Head scarves
Dombala: A Weegor guitar
Jin: Evil spirits
Yatak: Dorm room
Rah met: Thank you